P9-BWX-090

The Triplets Go South

The Triplets Go South

by
BERTHA B. MOORE

FOURTH IN THE SERIES

WM. B. EERDMANS PUBLISHING COMPANY
Grand Rapids 1954 **Michigan**

THE TRIPLETS GO SOUTH
by Bertha B. Moore

———————

Set up and printed, September, 1940

Tenth printing, December, 1954

This
BAER STORY
is
Lovingly Dedicated
to
ALICE EVELYN MADDREY

CONTENTS

The Triplets Go South

1

THE DECISION

TEDDY BAER motioned in a most mysterious manner to his sisters, Iona and Iva, to follow him. Very quietly, so as not to disturb Mother Baer, who was taking a nap on the couch in the living room, Iona and Iva tiptoed from the room. Teddy led the way to the back porch.

"Sit down here, you two. We have to decide something," he said, still in a most mysterious way.

Silently the girl triplets sat down, one on either side of Teddy, who had seated himself upon the top step of the porch.

"What in the world do we have to decide?" asked Iona.

"That's what I'd like to know," added Iva. "Is it very important?"

"It's just about the most important decision we've ever had to make," Teddy said, hugging his knees and looking off to the garden spot.

"Well, hurry and tell us, Teddy," coaxed Iona.

"Do hurry, Teddy. What is it about?" asked Iva.

"You know that letter Mother got from Aunt Mary?" Teddy asked his sisters, without looking at either one of them.

"Yes," they answered together.

"Well, you know she invited us to come down to Florida and spend our Easter vacation there. And you know how Mother and Daddy just sorta smiled about it and looked at each other as they do sometimes when they think they have a secret?" continued Teddy.

The girls nodded, and said, "Yes."

"I thought right away what a lot of fun it would be to go to Florida, but I never supposed for a single solitary minute we could go," Teddy began again.

"Oh, are we going?" cried Iona.

"Just you wait. I don't know. That's what we've got to decide. It's this way. A little while ago before Mother went to sleep, she and Daddy were talking together. Now, I didn't mean to listen, not the least bit. But how could I help hearing what they were saying when I was sitting in the swing right by the window on the front porch? I couldn't help it, could I?"

"No, you couldn't," agreed Iona.

"Of course, if you just kept on sitting in the swing, you couldn't. Of course, you could have gone on away. But of course, if you heard them begin to say something that needed deciding by us, you just had to stay. Hurry up, Teddy. What did you hear?" asked Iva.

"They were talking about Aunt Mary's letter. Mother was saying that she did wish we could go. She said she would feel a lot better satisfied if we were down there for those days. She wanted Daddy to take us in the car and come right straight back without us. He said he would not leave her when she wasn't feeling very well. So I thought it was settled and we were not going. Then Daddy said that Mr. Thompson was going to Florida on Thursday and couldn't we go with him. I got all excited and 'most jumped through the window. Mother didn't say anything for a little while. Then she said she hated to bother Mr. Thompson with three Baers on such a long trip. Daddy said he wouldn't mind. Then Mother said, how would we get back. Then the old telephone had to ring and I didn't hear another word. Daddy had to hurry to the office for something and Mother went to sleep. So that's what it is. Now, what do you say about going with Mr. Thompson? Would you girls be good and not bother him? And how could we get back? Of course, Daddy wouldn't want to come after us if he won't leave Mother to take us down there. Or don't you want to go?"

"Oh, I think it would be wonderful!" exclaimed Iona, softly.

"I'm like Daddy. I hate to leave Mother," said Iva, more gently. "Suppose, well, you know what, and she would need us and we'd be away off down in Florida? Then what?"

"Oh, but Aunt Lillie is coming tomorrow!" exclaimed Iona. "And she could have our room, if she wanted it instead of the company room."

"But the question is, will you girls not bother Mr. Thompson?" Teddy asked again.

"Why, Teddy Baer! Of course, we'll not bother Mr. Thompson any more than you will. The very idea!" was what Iona said.

"Well, I won't either. So there! Now, if we got down there, how could we get home. Mr. Thompson is going on to Miami, and it's a long ways from St. Augustine, because I looked on the road map. And he isn't coming back till next month," stated Teddy.

The girls sighed.

Then Iva said, slowly, "I guess we could come back on the train or on the bus. We went to Grandpa Baer's one time all by ourselves when we were not as old as we are now. That was a whole lot farther away than Florida is. Couldn't we come back alone, Teddy?"

"Of course we could!" instantly agreed Iona, before Teddy could say a word.

"Yes, we could. I honestly hadn't thought about that before. Why, we could come on the bus as easy as not. Wouldn't you girls rather come on the bus because we've never been on a bus and we have on a train," suggested Teddy, hopefully.

"I would. Or in an airplane," replied Iona.

Iva shook her head. "I don't want to come in an airplane. I'd like a bus ride. Teddy, let's come back in a bus!"

"Well! But how shall I get all this said to Mother and Daddy? You see, they may think it was just terrible for me to listen when I wasn't supposed to be listening, maybe. It's awfully impolite to listen to people talking when they don't know you are listening."

"Well, Teddy, just tell them exactly how it all happened, and they will understand. They always do. We've got the understandingest Mother and Daddy in the whole world!" declared Iona.

"All right! As soon as Daddy comes home, I'll tell him all by himself first. Then he'll know what to tell Mother. We mustn't worry her a bit, you know," he added, thoughtfully.

"I hate going away right now," said Iva, slowly.

"But Mother said she would feel ever so much better if we were not here for the next few days, Iva. It will be helping her if we go," reminded Teddy.

Iva sighed. Then she said, "Well, all right. If Daddy says it's best, I'll go, and I'll be as good as good."

"Do you suppose we'd better go pack our suitcases?" asked Iona.

"Of course not, silly!" Teddy told her. "We'll have plenty of time for that. This is only Tuesday. Mr. Thompson isn't going till Thursday, right after dinner. We'll have plenty of time to pack our suitcases."

"Here comes Daddy!" exclaimed Iona.

2

FOUR TO GO

"NOW you girls stay here and let me tell Daddy what we've decided. Then if you see me put my hand behind me and wave it to you, you come a scooting. It'll mean everything is all right," suggested Teddy, as he slid off the porch steps.

While he was gone, Iona said, "We'd better pray while he talks to Daddy. It always helps when we ask the Lord Jesus what to do."

"Yes, we had!" agreed Iva, and closed her eyes.

The girl triplets whispered their prayers and then opened their eyes to watch their brother. He had run to his father, who was closing the garage doors. The sisters saw their father stop and listen closely to what Teddy was saying. Then, suddenly, they jumped from their places and raced to Teddy's side. He had waved towards them with his hand behind his back!

"The girls said they'd not bother Mr. Thompson a bit, Daddy," Teddy was saying.

"We won't, Daddy! Really, truly, we'll be the best girls you ever saw!" promised Iona.

"We'll try to be awfully good, Daddy," promised Iva, a little more slowly.

"And I'll not bother him either," agreed Teddy.

"May we come back on the bus, Daddy?" asked Iona, eagerly.

Iva listened with both her ears and her two eyes and her mouth.

"Well, I suppose you'd have to come home some way and by bus would be as safe and good as any," their father said, but rather slowly and undecidedly.

"Oh, goody!" squealed Iona.

"Wait a minute!" warned her father. "We haven't seen Mr. Thompson yet and we haven't asked your mother what she thinks about it."

"But Daddy, what do you think?" asked Iona.

"I think it's a first rate plan, myself," he told her, and smiled his broadest.

"Then Mother will think so, too!" decided Iva, as the four Baers started towards the house.

At the kitchen Daddy Baer said, "Suppose you cubs let me go talk to your mother a little minute. I'll whistle for you if you are to come."

They agreed. Then they sat very still in the hall, listening for his whistle.

"I just know she'll say yes!" whispered Iona, and shivered with glee.

"I believe she will, too!" Iva whispered, and hugged her sister.

"Keep still, you girls!" Teddy whispered, leaning forward. "How do you expect us to hear Daddy whistle if you make so much noise?"

But they did hear him. Away they dashed to their mother's room.

"Are we going?" asked Iona and Teddy in one breath.

Iva waited, looking lovingly at her mother, who was sitting in a comfortable rocking chair, smiling a pleased and happy smile.

"We have decided to talk it over with Mr. Thompson. If he is willing to have three young Baer cubs along with him, your mother and I are willing to let you go to your Aunt Mary's for the Easter vacation," Daddy Baer said, and smiled a big, hearty, man-smile.

"Oh, Mother! We'll be the nicest Baers he ever did see!" declared Iona, kissing her mother's cheek.

"We'll mind every thing he says," promised Iva, squeezing her mother's hand.

"I'll go to see Mr. Thompson this evening. Your going depends upon him," their father said.

"We'll pray and pray that he'll say yes!" Iona exclaimed.

Later, while Daddy Baer was visiting Mr. Thompson, Iona and Iva were in their room, praying that Mr. Thompson would say yes. Teddy was out in the back yard, near the garage where he would see his father the very first minute he arrived home. He, too, was praying.

Daddy Baer did not visit Mr. Thompson very long. He was back so soon that Teddy was afraid that the going-to-Florida gentleman had not been home. He waited for the Baer car to be driven into the garage.

"What did he say?" Teddy asked, as his father alighted.

"Well, Teddy, my boy, he was as delighted as you three cubs have been. He said he would enjoy the trip much more with you children as companions than he would have going alone. So I suppose it is all settled," remarked Daddy Baer, as he started towards the house with his arm across Teddy's shoulders. "And you be sure to take good care of your sisters."

"Oh, I will, Daddy!" promised Teddy, willingly.

At the kitchen door they were met by the girls.

"Oh, he said yes, didn't he, Daddy? I can tell by the way Teddy looks," cried Iona.

"He said yes!" Teddy told them, because he just couldn't wait for his father to break the good news.

"Goody! Goody! Goody!" cried Iona and Iva, as they ran towards the living room. Their mother was waiting in there.

"He said yes, Mother!" cried Iona, bursting in first.

"Mother, will you get very lonesome?" asked Iva, thoughtfully, as she went more quietly up to her mother.

Mother Baer drew Iva close to her side. She said, "I'll be a little bit lonesome, but I am so glad that Mr. Thompson is willing to take you to St. Augustine. That is very accommodating of him."

Is it any wonder that the next day Iona missed three words in her spelling, that Teddy simply could not work one of his arithmetic problems, and that Iona said it was Jefferson who had crossed the Delaware? Would noon never come? Why didn't the bell ring to "take up" again? Then, how long the afternoon was! But finally even the longest days must end and the Baer Triplets were at home.

"Mother, hadn't we better pack?" asked Iona, the very first thing.

"It might be a good idea. Two young ladies and a young gentleman who are going to spend a few days in Florida will need to take along some clean garments, their bathing suits, their Sunday clothes, and their sleeping garments. So get busy!" she replied, smiling.

Out ran the Three Baers to do their packing. Oh, wasn't it the most fun! Neither Daddy Baer nor Mother Baer ran out with them. The older Baers believed in teaching their triplets to do things for themselves.

"Don't forget your bathing suits," Teddy reminded his sisters, as he disappeared into his own room.

"We won't!" promised Iona, as she gave Iva a gentle shove into their door. "It does seem funny to be packing bathing suits when it is still a little bit cold up here. It gives me the shivers to think of water."

"Maybe it'll be hot in Florida," Iona said, chuckling with delight, as she took her suitcase down from its shelf. "Here's yours, Iva," she added, handing the other suitcase to her sister.

Iva called across the hall to Teddy, "Don't forget to take your best socks, Ted!"

"And a lot of clean shirts and clean handkerchiefs!" Iona added.

"Same to you!" called back Teddy, which made the girls giggle.

"We'll wear our new dresses to Sunday school in Florida, because I just know Aunt Mary will go to church and Sunday school," Iona said, as she packed busily.

"I like Aunt Lillie's name the best," began Iva. "Isn't it funny how she got her name? She was born on Easter and they named her Lillie. I think it's nice. Don't you?"

"I think it's just beautiful. If I have any children born on Christmas or the Fourth of July, or some day like that, I'm going to name them Holly or Independence or such like!" replied Iona, as she laid another print frock on her bed.

"So'm I!" Iva said, without actually knowing what she was saying, because she was trying to fit her Sunday shoes into a very small space.

Teddy presently appeared in the doorway and announced, "I'm all packed!"

"Did you put everything in carefully, Ted?" asked Iona, looking at him in a very big-sisterly manner.

"Of course I did! Do you suppose I just stuffed 'em in? We men don't have as many silly frills and things as you girls have," he said, as he held his head high and started, whistling softly, towards the living room.

He found his mother and father talking about the trip.

Back in the girls' room, Iona was exclaiming, "There!" as she squeezed the lid down on her suitcase. "I can't get in another single solitary thing."

"Neither can I!" announced Iva, as she pressed hers together with her knee. "I hope we haven't left out anything important."

They joined the other Baers then in the living room.

"Your cousin Rosemary must be a very beautiful child," Mother Baer said to her three husky triplets. "I hope you will try to be very polite and considerate of her and your Aunt Mary and Uncle Bill. It has been a long time since they have seen any of us and I want them to love my Three Baers. If they find our children beautifully behaved they will have better opinions of their parents."

"O Mother, we'll be simply perfect!" quickly declared Iona.

"We'll do our very best," added Iva. "We'll never ask for a second helping of anything, not even ice cream. We'll say please and thank you and good-night and good-morning and God Bless You and all the nice things we can think of!"

"And I'll not slam the doors, or run through the house, or yell at the girls," was Teddy's promise.

Mother Baer looked as if she wanted to laugh, but she said, smiling sweetly at her young Baers, "If you remember all those things, I shall be well satisfied."

The trip was about all any one could talk about. It was after supper and bedtime before any one realized it. Said

Daddy Baer, with a big, healthy yawn, "Don't you think it's time to sleep a little while?"

Looking quite surprised, Iona said, "O Daddy! If you should yawn like that before Aunt Mary and Uncle Bill they would think you had frightful manners. You didn't set us a good example then."

Daddy Baer clapped his hand over his mouth quickly, and, chuckling, said, "Excuse me, please! And then don't ever try to copy my yawn. It's my own personal yawn."

Everyone laughed, and Mother Baer said, "Let's have our Bible reading and prayer now."

"Mother Baer, how would you like to hear your children repeat the Twenty-third Psalm for us tonight?" Daddy Baer wanted to know.

"I'd love it!" Mother Baer declared, as she leaned back in her big chair and closed her eyes while Teddy, Iona, and Iva stood very straight and repeated the beautiful Shepherd's Psalm, without a single slip. Then Daddy Baer asked the Lord Jesus to care for them through the night, to bless all who were tired and cold and hungry, and to have mercy on the whole world. He prayed for three missionaries whom they knew. He prayed for the Jews everywhere. Then he prayed again especially for Mother Baer who was not very well.

As she was leaving the room, Iva whispered to her mother, "God will take care of you, Mother," and then kissed her.

"Yes, my darling, I know He will. And He will take care of my three dear children and Mr. Thompson as they all roll along on the highways," her mother said.

"Isn't it nice, Mother, to know that God will be seeing us and you and Daddy all at the same time!" Iona said, as she kissed her mother good-night.

"Yes, it is, my sweet. How comforting it is to all who have sons and daughters in dangerous places to know that God sees and cares and knows all about them."

"Like mothers who have sons in the awful war in Europe," added Teddy, as he waited, hoping his mother would kiss him, too, since he was going to leave her for a few days.

"Yes, my son, like them!" she said, as she held her hands out to him. "I'm glad you are only twelve years old," she whispered, as she kissed him.

"Good-night, Mother! Good-night, Daddy!" called the Three Baers.

Tomorrow they were starting to Florida!

They would see the Atlantic ocean!

They might even put on their bathing suits and get all wet in the ocean!

3

OFF TO THE SOUTH

WHO, expecting to start to Florida soon after lunch, could sit still in a school room and apply himself very strictly to the lessons all morning long?

Not Iona Baer!

Not Teddy Baer!

Not even Iva Baer!

They tried. Yes, indeed! But right in the middle of the arithmetic class Iona was writing the word "Florida." When Teddy was supposed to be studying his history lesson, he really was trying to figure out how many miles it was to St. Augustine. When Iva was trying to think up a complex-compound sentence, she was wondering what her Cousin Rosemary really was like.

The watch in Teddy's pocket ticked away so very slowly. When the twelve o'clock bell finally rang, how very beautiful it did sound!

"I hope you will have a delightful time!" said Miss Allbrite, their attractive teacher, as the Three Baers left her

26

room. "Be sure to be able to tell us about everything you see."

"We will!" the three promised at once.

They ran towards the street as fast as their legs could carry them. For once Iona and Iva beat Teddy, but it was because a boy stopped him. The boy wanted Teddy to send him some picture postcards from the Atlantic Ocean.

"Here you are!" called out Mr. Thompson, in a cheery greeting. "You girls jump in the back. Teddy may ride up here with me."

For a fleeting minute the girls were shy and even homesick for their mother. Iona wondered if she were all right. Iva just knew she should have remained at home. Teddy was beginning to enjoy his trip even then.

"I suppose you are three very hungry Baers," remarked Mr. Thompson, as he started his big car on its journey south.

The girls looked at each other and waited. Really, they had not thought about being hungry. They hoped Teddy would say something, for when eating was mentioned, they discovered they were hungry.

"It is noon!" was Teddy's remark.

"And most folks eat at noon," said Mr. Thompson. "Well, I've already had my lunch. When I stopped at your house for your suitcases, your mother and Aunt

Lillie, who is a very lovely woman, insisted that I eat some lunch before I left them. So, I'm not very hungry!"

Iona and Iva looked again at each other, and waited. Teddy also was waiting.

Iona whispered, "Say something!" to Iva.

And Iva said, "Yes, sir!"

Teddy cleared his throat and tried to be natural as he added, "We'll be seeing so many new sights that we'll soon forget we are hungry."

Mr. Thompson laughed right out as if it was a good joke.

"You are pretty brave young cubs," he said. "Teddy, suppose you open that box beside you. I think there must be something to eat in it."

"Oh!" cried Iona, eagerly, as she leaned over Teddy's shoulder.

"Yummy-yum!" said Iva, when she saw the beautiful sandwiches and fruit and cookies.

"Your Aunt Lillie said that you might be able to put a little of that away. While we are still in the city where you know the sights, you might nibble a few bites. Then when we are out in the country that is new, you may watch what goes outside," suggested Mr. Thompson.

Nibble a few bites! They were hungry! Even Mr. Thompson ate some more. Before long the box was emptied.

"We'd better not throw away the box in the streets, had we?" asked Teddy.

"What do you think?" Mr. Thompson asked Teddy, instead of replying to his question.

"I shouldn't want empty boxes thrown in the street in front of my house," Teddy said. "I'll save it till we get out in the country where there are no houses in sight. Maybe no one will care then."

"It's a nice box. Let's save it for some other time," said Iva.

So the box was not cast from the window.

The farther they went the better they liked being with Mr. Thompson. He knew all about the states through which he was driving. He knew a good many amusing stories to tell. They all laughed and laughed, and so did Mr. Thompson.

As they were driving through Georgia, Teddy asked, "What are those funny-looking cups and buckets hanging to those pine trees for?"

"To catch turpentine!" replied Mr. Thompson.

"To catch turpentine!" exclaimed Teddy. "Where is the turpentine?"

"The next time we pass a patch of pines, I'll drive more slowly. Then you watch closely. You will notice that the bark of the tree has been removed in strips and that a sticky fluid is exuding from the strips. It is resin. This is taken to a refinery where it is made into turpentine," he told the interested triplets.

"Turpentine that we put on bruises and cuts?" asked Teddy.

"The very same! It is used as a medicine and some that is a little different is used in paints. It all comes from these pine trees."

"The next time I use some turpentine, I'll think of these pretty pine trees," said Iona, laughing.

"I'll think of Georgia," added Iva.

"North Carolina is called the Turpentine State. Then these pines grow in Florida and South Carolina and other states."

After a little while Mr. Thompson said, "I have to stop in Waycross to see a man. You may all get out and stretch your legs, but don't go wandering off from the car too far. It won't take me very long."

"Mr. Thompson, could we buy something to eat?" asked Teddy, shyly, yet hopefully.

The girls giggled. How they did hope he would give his permission!

Mr. Thompson looked at all three as if he were trying to decide what to reply. Then, laughing, he said, "I declare, I never saw three Baers who looked hungrier. You certainly may buy some food. Have you any money?"

"Oh, yes!" quickly replied Teddy. "We each have a dollar to spend on the trip down."

"A dollar! That's a lot of money, especially when there are three of them. You aren't there, yet, remember. We'll have to camp somewhere tonight and have something to eat when we camp and some breakfast. Suppose you budget your dollars!" Mr. Thompson told them.

"I'll budget my dollar!" thought Iona.

Mr. Thompson stopped the car in front of a handsome grocery store. He told the Triplets, "There is a drug store on the corner. A ten cent store is between it and this grocery store. I may be gone an hour. The car will be right here."

Then he was gone!

The Three Baers sat still and held a consultation.

"What'll we buy?" asked Iona.

"Fruit!" decided Teddy. "Let's not eat candy. You know how Mother always says candy isn't very good for us on trips and we don't want to be sick when we get to Aunt Mary's house. Those are grand looking oranges. Let's get some oranges and —" he hesitated.

"And some graham crackers," suggested Iona.

"I'm already thirsty," announced Iva. "I'd rather have a drink."

"Well, let's go to the drug store and have a chocolate milk. Then we'll come back and get some oranges. How's that?" asked Teddy.

"Grand!" exclaimed Iona and Iva.

When Mr. Thompson returned, he found the Triplets again in the car, eating oranges.

"They are the best oranges I ever ate," declared Teddy.

"We saved you some," Iona told him.

"Hurrah! How about some peanuts? Did you have any while I was gone?"

They shook their heads, while Teddy replied, "We forgot about peanuts."

"Good citizens of Georgia would never forget peanuts," laughingly Mr. Thompson said, as he gave each one of the triplets a bag of the peanuts.

"Oh, thank you, Mr. Thompson!" exclaimed the girls, while Teddy thanked him also.

"And now off we go again!" said the driver, as he headed south.

"When do we reach Florida?" asked Iona.

"We are very near there now. Shall we stop at a tourist camp for the night or go on till we reach St. Augustine long after dark? If we camp we shall be seeing the ocean in the morning and can drive along the ocean front a few miles. If we go on now, it will be dark and you won't be able to see the Atlantic."

"Let's stay at a tourist camp!" said Iona. "We never did stay all night at one."

"Do let's!" Iva added.

"Do you third the motion?" Mr. Thompson asked Teddy.

"Yes, sir, I do! I don't want to miss seeing the ocean as soon as we can."

"That's settled then. The first camp that looks clean and comfortable will have three Baers and a Thompson as all night guests."

After a little while Mr. Thompson said, "I can almost smell the ocean."

"Smell the ocean!" Teddy exclaimed, "What does it smell like?"

"Salt!"

"Salt!" cried Iona. "I didn't know you could smell salt."

"When you reach the Atlantic tomorrow, you will discover that salt does have an odor," Mr. Thompson told them.

A few minutes later Teddy gave a frightened scream. Mr. Thompson jammed on his brakes, causing Iona and Iva to bump their heads. He began to make the car go backwards.

"Did you hit him?" cried Teddy.

"Who?" asked Iona and Iva, frightened.

"An old man!" Teddy told them.

"I think I did not hit him. I think he just fell as we came up even with him. I certainly hope I didn't hit him," Mr. Thompson said, in a queer voice.

He stopped the car and jumped out. Teddy got out, too. The girls opened their door and stood on the running board, watching.

On the shoulder of the highway lay an old man, apparently unconscious. Mr. Thompson was examining him.

"I didn't hit him!" he announced, and sounded relieved. "He must have fainted. Teddy, get me some water from the jug. One of you girls give me a handkerchief. The other one squeeze some orange juice in a paper cup and have it ready for him. That's all I have to give him as a stimulant."

The triplets worked fast. Mr. Thompson bathed the old man's face with the cold water. Presently the closed eyes began to flutter.

"He's coming to. Now get the orange juice ready," directed Mr. Thompson.

Iva stood with the cup of orange juice in her hand. The old man opened his eyes.

"Drink this, Grandpa," said Mr. Thompson, tenderly, as he held the cup of juice to the old lips.

The old man drank the juice and looked about him.

"That's good!" he mumbled. "Hungry!"

"Oh!" exclaimed Iona and Iva.

The old man was hungry!

A car stopped. A man came towards Mr. Thompson, who was kneeling beside the old man.

"Did you hit him?" asked the stranger.

"No, sir, I did not!" declared Mr. Thompson, gladly. "He fainted just as I passed him. He is coming to and says he is hungry."

"I'm a doctor. Let me have a look at him. I'll get my case and be right back."

The strange doctor backed his car till it was behind Mr. Thompson's. Then he jumped out and was quickly beside the old man, who was murmuring words no one quite understood. The doctor examined him with skillful hands.

"He is hungry. Where are you going?" asked the doctor of Mr. Thompson.

"We are on our way to St. Augustine. We had planned to stop at the first tourist camp."

"You folks go on. Help me get him into my car. I live in the next town and I'll take care of him. It's a good thing you passed just when you did."

Mr. Thompson helped the doctor place the feeble old man in his car. Then once again he started south.

"Poor old man!" said Teddy, with a sigh.

"Yes, it is a pity that an old man like him is ever allowed on the highway, but perhaps he has no home. Not all the suffering in the world is being endured in Europe and

Asia. There is a good deal of it right here at home," sadly said Mr. Thompson.

"I hope he has a good supper," Iona murmured.

"And a good bed," added Iva.

"He will. That doctor seemed like a kind man," Mr. Thompson assured them. Then, coming upon a tourist camp, he asked, "How do you like the looks of this place?"

They all liked it and presently they were in a two-room cabin with a stove in one room and a table with dishes and cooking utensils on it.

"We can cook!" cried Iona.

"I'm a good cook!" announced Mr. Thompson.

What a time they had! Teddy and Mr. Thompson went to the little camp store and brought back bread and bacon and eggs and milk and lettuce. Iva discovered tomatoes in another sack. And even as they ate, they became sleepy.

"Early to bed so we can have an early morning start," suggested Mr. Thompson.

"Aren't we going to have our prayer and verses?" asked Iva.

Mr. Thompson looked at her as if he didn't understand fully what she meant.

Teddy explained, "You see, Mr. Thompson, every night we say some Bible verses and then Daddy prays. Shall we do that tonight?"

"By all means! I've been a member of the church for years and years and I pray sometimes when trouble comes, but, well, I've never really known any one who consistently read his Bible and prayed. I'm glad to know you do."

Each of the Triplets repeated a Bible verse. Then Teddy prayed, asking the dear Lord Jesus to take care of their mother and father and the poor old man. He did not forget to give thanks for the safe journey of the afternoon and to thank Him for a friend like Mr. Thompson.

And right away it was morning! In no time at all the bacon was frying, the oranges were "juiced," and the eggs were scrambled. And in no time at all the food had disappeared and the mess all cleared away.

"All aboard for the great Atlantic ocean!" called Mr. Thompson, as he stepped on the starter.

"Let's see who'll smell salt first!" exclaimed Teddy, sniffing.

4

THE ATLANTIC OCEAN

"WHERE is the Atlantic ocean?" Iona wanted to know, as they kept driving along and did not see any ocean.

"It's out there to the left of you about thirty miles," Mr. Thompson told her. "When we reach Jacksonville, we'll be nearer it. We shall likely have to go much nearer St. Augustine before we have a full view of it."

"Let's hurry!" Iona sighed, settling back into her corner.

Presently they were in Jacksonville.

"This is a BIG city!" Teddy remarked. "It has a lot of traffic."

Mr. Thompson was too busy watching the stop-and-go signals to do much talking and the young Baers were too busy watching the people, the car tags from many states, and the stores. Then, right in the very center of one of the very busiest streets, when Mr. Thompson stopped at a red signal, the engine flopped and would not start the first time he stepped on the starter. Mr. Thompson tried again. There was no murmur from the starter! Cars behind began to honk impatiently. The traffic policeman motioned for him to move. But how could he? The cars honked louder and constantly. Mr. Thompson's face became very red.

"Are we out of gas?" asked Teddy, anxiously.

"No, there is plenty of gas. I don't know what is wrong. This has never happened to this car before!" replied Mr. Thompson, as anxiously as Teddy had.

"Will we have to stay here?" Iona wanted to know.

The traffic officer motioned for the cars to come on around the stalled car. Then he started towards Mr. Thompson.

"Oh, will he arrest us?" whispered Iva, frightened.

But the officer asked kindly, "What's the trouble?"

"Unless the starter is hanging, I don't know," replied Mr. Thompson, as he wiped his forehead with his handkerchief. "There is plenty of gas."

"We'll roll you to the curb and investigate," said the obliging policeman, as he motioned to two men who were watching to come and help.

When the car was at the curb, the men "jiggled" it back and forth until all of a sudden there was a little click and the starter was all right.

"There you are!" said the traffic officer.

While Iona and Iva and Teddy sighed with gratitude, Mr. Thompson thanked the policeman and the men who had helped. Away they started again.

"I hope that doesn't happen any more," Mr. Thompson said, when he was safely in line behind a good many cars all headed for the same bridge. "But we've learned what to do if it does!"

"We've had another experience," remarked Iona. "Last night it was the poor old man and today it was the poor old car."

They were upon a long, high bridge.

"Oh, is that the Atlantic ocean?" exclaimed Iona.

"No, this is the St. Johns river. We have to cross this river in order to continue south and east to St. Augustine," Mr. Thompson said.

"How far away is St. Augustine now?" asked Teddy

"It's about thirty miles."

"Can you smell the ocean yet, Mr. Thompson?" Iva wanted to know.

Mr. Thompson laughingly told her he was beginning to believe he could. He sniffed. All three of the Baers sniffed.

"I can smell it!" announced Iona.

"I can't!" declared Iva.

"I can!" exclaimed Teddy.

"How does it smell?" asked Mr. Thompson.

"It smells clean and fresh and salty!" replied Teddy.

"I can't smell it, but I know I'm getting warmer. I hope it is hot in St. Augustine so we can go in bathing," Iva said.

"Let's go in even if it is cold," suggested Teddy, to which the girls agreed.

Presently Teddy asked, "Mr. Thompson, aren't you even a little bit hungry?"

Very seriously he looked at Teddy. Then he said, "Come to think of it, I believe I am. It isn't late enough for lunch yet, though. We should be in St. Augustine in time for lunch. I'll stop at the next filling station and telephone your Aunt Mary. She may tell us what to do about eating."

As the car stopped, the Three Baers saw a sign that said St. Augustine was only five more miles. They were delighted.

Said Teddy, with a sigh, while Mr. Thompson was telephoning, "As hungry as we are it is going to be dreadfully hard to remember all our best manners."

"Teddy Baer, don't you dare disgrace your parents!" Iona warned him.

"Aren't you girls hungry, too? Iona said she was," Teddy wanted to know.

"Yes, we are, but we are going to be polite, even if we are. We are going to show how well we have been taught so Aunt Mary and Uncle Bill will respect our parents," Iva reminded him.

"Oh, well, I'll be as polite as you girls are, any time," retorted Teddy, just as Mr. Thompson returned.

"She says she is expecting you and to come right on to her house for lunch. She says she will wait till one o'clock for you."

"It's only five more miles," Teddy told him, as the car started on its journey.

"And it is only eleven o'clock. Do you suppose you might need some nourishment in order to appear your best when you do arrive?" asked Mr. Thompson, as he glanced at each one of his guests.

"We are hungry, but we can wait," politely replied Iona.

"But a little something, say, such as a tangerine, might help?" he asked Teddy.

Teddy smiled broadly, saying, "Oh, yes, Mr. Thompson, but we can wait."

"Reach in my pocket and get those tangerines, Teddy. I think your morale will be strengthened with food," laughingly Mr. Thompson said.

How good those tangerines were! Suddenly Iona almost choked as she exclaimed, "Oh, look! There's the Atlantic ocean!"

The car began to go more slowly. All four occupants looked and sniffed.

"Is that Europe across there?" asked Iva, pointing to land.

"Take a good look at what you are seeing," Mr. Thompson told them. "This is a broad strip of water, the broadest you have likely ever seen. However, it is not the Atlantic. You are looking at Matanzas bay. The body of land is Anastasia island. Beyond the island is the ocean.

Before you can see the real ocean from the main land, you will have to be taken farther down the coast."

With a disappointed sigh, Iona said, "Oh, I thought this was the ocean and we were seeing Europe!"

"Why, silly!" cried Teddy. "Don't you know your geography any better than that? The Atlantic ocean is miles and miles and miles wide and no one can see Europe from this side."

"I guess I wasn't really thinking," acknowledged Iona. "I hoped we might be seeing Europe, but I didn't want to hear the bombs."

Mr. Thompson asked, "How would you like to cross over to the island and take a swift glimpse of the ocean before we run on to your aunt's? If she will wait till one o'clock, we shall have time."

"Oh, let's!" they all exclaimed.

They passed everything exciting with no comment, for they were watching the high bridge that connected St. Augustine and the island. Presently they were upon it and could see nothing but water beneath them.

"That was The Bridge of Lions," Mr. Thompson told them, as he began the drive of seven miles on to St. Augustine Beach. "It is built of concrete and steel and is a draw bridge, the draw being raised to allow the shrimp boats to pass. As we return, notice the two marble lions at the entrance of the city. I think you can see them."

"I saw them!" announced Iona and Iva together.

"So did I!" Teddy added. Then he asked, "What are shrimp, Mr. Thompson?"

"A shrimp is a small shell-fish that must be about a first cousin to a lobster. And here we are at the Atlantic ocean!"

The Three Baers jumped from the car. They stood beside Mr. Thompson, shading their eyes while they gazed far, far, far out to the horizon. Away out there the water looked as smooth as the pavement over which they had come. But near the shore the water was dashing and splashing, sending spray over the rocks and upon the sand. For a short moment no one spoke.

"The Atlantic ocean!" finally Iona murmured, her voice full of awe. "I knew it would be big, but this looks as if it covered half the whole wide word. It almost frightens me."

"I don't think I want to go out in it," Iva said, quietly.

"I do!" stoutly declared Teddy. "Those people look as if it is fun.

"Suppose one of those great big waves would swallow you?" exclaimed Iva.

"They aren't swallowing those folks. I'm going in if I get a chance," their brother repeated, as the three turned back to the car.

As they neared the bridge, Mr. Thompson said, "Look! The draw is opened to allow that little boat to pass. Watch it close again for us."

They watched as the center sections of the great bridge came slowly together. Down the Bay went the little boat.

"Maybe it is full of shrimps," suggested Iona. "Did you ever eat any shrimp, Mr. Thompson?"

"Yes, I like fried shrimp very much. And now take a look at old St. Augustine, the oldest city in the whole United States of America. We'll not have time to see much, for it is about one o'clock."

No one talked. They didn't have time. They were too busy watching everything. Presently Mr. Thompson said, "We are on the street now. Watch for 1856, which is the number of your Aunt Mary's house."

"That's it!" spied Iona. "That white house there on the corner!"

5

ROSEMARY, DARLING!

IONA, Iva, and Teddy Baer suddenly felt rather shy. It had been while they were yet very small triplets that Aunt Mary and Uncle Bill had visited them. They had never seen their cousin, Rosemary. And now, here they were, stepping from the shelter of the friendly car, right at the front door!

And out upon the porch came a lady who did look a little like Mother Baer. Beside her, holding to her hand, was a little girl. Suddenly that little girl darted into the house, out of sight!

"Come in!" called Aunt Mary, as she went to meet the visitors.

"This is Mr. Thompson, Aunt Mary," said Teddy, who had been told exactly what to do. "This is our Aunt Mary Stevens, Mr. Thompson."

When the introductions were over, Iona picked up her suitcase, Iva picked up her suitcase, and Teddy picked up his suitcase and they all followed Aunt Mary Stevens into the house.

"Rosemary darling, come here, dear!" Aunt Mary called, up the stairs.

"I don't want to!" answered a little voice.

Iona and Iva exchanged surprised glances.

"She is just a little bashful," her mother said, as she smiled at her nieces and nephew. "And I know you are hungry. Just set your suitcases here in the hall. After lunch you may go to your rooms. Mr. Thompson, I am so glad you could bring the children for this little visit. I understand they are to start back on the early bus Monday morning?"

"That's right!" replied Mr. Thompson. "And now, I must start on my last lap of my trip on to Miami. I shall leave the Baers in your hands, Mrs. Stevens."

Mr. Thompson was going to leave them! Of course they had known this all along, but now it seemed to shock every Baer. They looked at him with real distress.

Mrs. Stevens said, "Oh, but Mr. Thompson, you must not think of going until after lunch. It is all ready and will be served at once. You girls run upstairs and wash your hands in the bathroom up there. It is the last door on your right. Teddy, you and Mr. Thompson will find a lavatory right in here. I'll go tell Clementine to serve lunch immediately." Then, as she started towards the kitchen while the guests were all seeking a place to freshen up a bit, she called again, "Rosemary darling! Come on down, dear!"

"Now darling!" her mother called, gently.

Iona whispered to Iva, as they bathed their faces and hands, "I wish she would come on and get acquainted. She can't be any more scared than we are."

"Yes, she can!" Iva told her sister. "There are three of us and only one of her. She looked right pretty, so little, and with her hair so fair and curly."

As the Three Baers took their places at the table, they waited. Mr. Thompson and Aunt Mary were there, but no Rosemary! Aunt Mary began to serve the food at once. She had not returned thanks as always was done in the Baer family! The food was good and the Triplets were hungry, but it did not seem exactly right to them. Iona and Iva said, "Thank Thee, Lord," in their hearts, and Teddy decided he would remember when he said his night prayers.

Presently in came Rosemary, looking a little sullen, the Baer sisters thought.

"Rosemary darling, here are your cousins, Iona and Iva and Teddy. Do be sweet and speak to them."

Without glancing at any of them, she said, "I don't want to!"

"Now darling!" her mother said, but very gently.

Rosemary darling took her place at the table. She looked at her plate. She said, "I don't want this old baked potato!"

Iona gulped. Iva almost dropped her fork. Teddy swallowed hard. What beautiful manners Rosemary did NOT have!

"What do you want, darling?" asked her mother.

"I want some orange sherbet!" announced the little miss.

Quietly Aunt Mary rang a little bell. In came a smiling Negro girl, Clementine!

"Please take this potato for the present and bring Rosemary some orange sherbet," said Mrs. Stevens.

"And some cake!" added little Miss Rosemary.

Teddy cast a sly glance at Mr. Thompson, but that gentleman was eating his baked Irish potato as if he enjoyed it. Teddy secretly wished he could go with Mr. Thompson. To be with his sisters was bad enough when he was away from home, but to be with three girls and one of them a little girl like his Cousin Rosemary, well! He was already glad Monday was not far off!

Not during the entire lunch did Rosemary make up with her cousins, although her mother made another attempt to persuade her to be pleasant to her guests. Soon Mr. Thompson was ready to go.

"We had the best trip ever we did," declared Iona, as she told him good-bye.

"Yes, we did. Thank you ever so much for letting us come with you. I hope we didn't bother you very much," Iva said, as she shook his hand.

"The pleasure is all mine. Any time I can take you three Baers some place again, please let me know. I'll be glad to have you. I am sorry you aren't going the rest of the way with me. I'll be lonesome now."

"We're sorry, too. I know I am. You were grand to us and we certainly thank you," Teddy told him.

Then he was gone. Rosemary had been standing beside her mother. She looked at her cousins.

"They are not bears!" she said, and looked at each one without smiling at all.

The Baers did smile. Said Iona, "That's our name, Rosemary. I'm Iona Baer. She's Iva Baer. He's Teddy Baer."

"It's not a pretty name," declared their dainty little cousin.

"We can't help that. It's the name we were born into," Iva told her, trying to be polite.

"What would you like to do this afternoon, children?" asked their Aunt Mary ."You are to be here for so short a time that you will have to crowd every hour of each day chock full of sights. Would you like to make a little tour over the oldest city in the nation and see some of the old buildings?"

"Oh, yes, if you please," replied Teddy, for all of them.

"I'm going along!" promptly said Rosemary.

"Certainly, Rosemary darling. Mother would not leave her little girl at home," sweetly replied Aunt Mary.

"I'd not stay!" declared Rosemary.

Her mother merely smiled and held out her hand to her. But Rosemary was in no notion of being held. She skipped lightly from the room.

Presently they were all on their way to see Old St. Augustine, Rosemary in the front seat with her mother, who was driving, and the triplets in the back seat.

"First we'll see old Fort Marion, which is the oldest fort that is left standing in our country. The very earliest forts were built of wood, but the enemies easily set fire to them. So this fort is made of a peculiar sort of stone that comes from the island. It is a mixture of shells and sand. It is called Coquina. It took nearly ninety years to build Fort Marion, for it was begun in 1670 and was not finished until 1756.

"Who built it?" asked Teddy.

"A good many different kinds of people had a part in its building, Teddy. There were Negro slaves, soldiers, and the inhabitants of the city, which at that time was a walled city. Finally the fort was named in honor of General Francis Marion of the Revolutionary War. He himself was from South Carolina," Aunt Mary said.

On the way to the Fort the visitors noticed the quaint old carriages with the courteous Negro drivers. They were standing at the various curbs, waiting for some one to see the Oldest City in the United States.

"I think it would be fun to ride in a carriage like that," said Iona, with a giggle.

"I don't! They're too slow and pokey!" retorted Rosemary.

Teddy seemed not to have heard his cousin's remark, for he asked, "Aunt Mary, why are there so many of them? The horses are pretty."

"Some of these carriages are the old hacks. The drivers are guides who take visitors with plenty of time and who enjoy riding leisurely to see our city. See that rock before you? It is the Zero Milestone. It marks the eastern end of the first transcontinental highway that went from St. Augustine to San Diego in California."

The rock looked like a huge globe, except that it did not have a map of the world upon it.

"What's trans-con-tin-en-tial, Mummy?" asked Rosemary.

"Let's see if Teddy knows, darling," suggested her mother.

"I don't want to see if Teddy knows, I want to see if you know, Mummy."

"It means all the way across the nation, Rosemary darling. I do wish you would be a sweet little girl," her mother replied, rather sadly.

"I am a sweet little girl!" answered Rosemary.

Teddy nudged his sisters.

On the way to the side of the Fort where she wanted to park her car, Aunt Mary said, as she pointed up the highway, "At the end of this street are the gates to the city.

The old wall that once protected the little city, has been taken away, but the gates still stand."

"Oh! We passed through them when we came into St. Augustine!" Teddy remembered.

Aunt Mary drew up at the curb. As she did so, Rosemary whimpered, "I want some ice cream!"

For once her mother did not yield to her want. Instead she said, "Not right this minute, darling. You see, children, the Spanish, the French, and the English all fought for this very spot before the Americans ever were here. These outer walls are twelve feet thick at the base and taper to seven at the top. There is only this one entrance. There are thirty-one rooms inside. In the center is an open court. From the top one can get a wonderful view of the city and the bay," Aunt Mary explained, while Rosemary tried to whine petulantly. Seeing that she accomplished nothing, she followed slowly where her mother led the visiting cousins.

"I don't want to see this old Fort any more. I want to see the old house," finally Rosemary said, as she tugged at her mother's hand.

"All right, Rosemary darling. We'll take our guests to see the oldest house in America. Would you like that, children?"

Would they! It was one request their cousin made they did like.

Back to the car they went. This time Aunt Mary did not drive so very far. Presently she said, "Here we are!"

and stopped before a house that was built at the very edge of the sidewalk. There were great double doors at which each one paid twenty-five cents before entering. This money is used to preserve and take care of this historical house.

Before they entered, Aunt Mary told them to look at the walls. "This first floor is built of thick coquina. The upper story is of wood. These walls and fences hide the beautiful gardens, but we shall see them later. Now let's go inside."

What a strange, yet beautiful house!

"These floors are an inch thick," explained Aunt Mary. "Those beams are all of cedar and were hewn by hand. Not a single nail was used in building the original house. Wooden pegs were used instead."

"I want some cards!" announced Rosemary, going to a table where postcards, showing views of the old house, were for sale.

The Baers discovered they also wanted some cards.

There were so many things to see that the wishing well, the money vine, the old Spanish bed, the huge fireplace, and all the other antiques were jumbled together in the heads of the Three Baers.

Aunt Mary decided it was time to start home. On the way she stopped at a grocery store which was even more attractive than the one in Waycross. She asked the visiting Baers what they liked to eat. As if they could decide when there were so many delicious things before them!

"Shrimp!" decided Rosemary for them.

"We might like shrimps," Teddy said, politely.

And when the shrimps were fried crisp and good, all three of the visitors did enjoy them. And Uncle Bill! Well, he was the jolliest uncle they had, they believed before the dinner had ended. He took them across to Anastasia Island so they could look back to the lighted city. They were sleepy before they returned home, but not Rosemary! She was wide awake and wanting ice cream. Even Uncle Bill humored Rosemary! They stopped for ice cream!

In their own room as Iona and Iva prepared for bed, Iona said softly, "Rosemary is a little bit sweet. She makes me think of a little yellow soft, cuddly chicken like Grandmother Baer's. But isn't she the spoiled child!"

"I guess it's because she is an only," murmured Iva, sleepily.

"I'm glad I'm not an only," replied Iona, yawning.

"So'm I! I wonder how Mother is," she added, as she knelt beside her bed.

"The Lord Jesus will take care of her," Iona assured her, as she knelt beside Iva.

It seemed as if they had only jumped into bed when it was time to jump out again. At breakfast, when Rosemary was absent, the plan was made for Aunt Mary to pick up Uncle Bill at his office and then all go down to the sand dunes to Summer Haven, for a picnic.

Soon, clad in their bathing suits, the Three Baers and Rosemary, who appeared to be in a little better humor, were in the car with Aunt Mary and Uncle Bill on their way to take a dip in the Atlantic ocean!

Once at the beach, while Uncle Bill and Aunt Mary made camp, the children from the "north" ran after Rosemary into the water. At the edge, Iona and Iva stopped.

"It's cold!" they squealed.

Rosemary did not hesitate. Teddy was not to be outdone. He ran with her. Then, of course, with chattering teeth, Iona and Iva followed also. Soon the water was warmer, at least it seemed so. They had a happy time, racing and playing in the Atlantic ocean. Presently Uncle Bill took Teddy away out beyond the breakers where the water was smoother. He almost taught Teddy how to swim. Aunt Mary kept the girls nearer the shore. Presently Uncle Bill and Teddy came up to them, riding a huge wave.

"Do you girls want to try it?" Uncle Bill asked.

Now always what Teddy did, his sisters wanted to try, too. So first Iona and then Iva was taken out to see how it felt where the water was deep. Iona came back squealing with delight. But Iva was afraid. Instead of jumping at the right time, she opened her mouth to speak to her Uncle Bill and was strangled with the salt water. Uncle Bill held her up and kept her from being knocked down completely by the wave. Then he brought her quickly to the beach where she sputtered and coughed until all the water had left her lungs. But she didn't care. It was fun and she had been in the ocean.

When they had eaten the good lunch, and had dried thoroughly, the girls slipped on dresses, for they were to go visiting the alligators and ostriches! They saw Old Ponce, an alligator which was nine hundred years old.

"He isn't a bit pretty!" declared Rosemary.

"Maybe you'd not be pretty either if you were nine hundred years old," her cousin Teddy told her, and smiled so that she could not be offended.

They saw an ostrich swallow an orange. They saw the old moss-back alligator, and the peafowl with its beautiful tail and ugly feet. They saw so many strange sights that again their brains felt bemuddled, as Iona said.

Then it was time to go home. Every one was tired and the big car felt very comfortable as they settled back into their places.

6

ON A SUNDAY

AS IVA, Teddy and Iona descended the stairs on that Sunday morning, which was Easter Sunday, they were dressed in their "Sunday best." They heard their Aunt Mary talking to some one over the telephone. She was saying, "Oh, I am so glad! Congratulations from all of us! They are getting along the very best ever. Yes, we'll send them home in the morning."

The Three Baers stopped still. Was Aunt Mary talking to their father? Was their mother ill?

"Yes, I understand. No, I won't. All right, don't you worry at all. We shall see that they are on the seven o'clock bus and you meet it when it gets in at nine. Didn't you say nine? I wish I were coming with them. We can't right now. I don't want Rosemary to miss school. The little darling has had to miss so much because she was sick such a long time. We do hope we can come this vacation, though. I wouldn't miss coming now for a good deal. Give Sis my best love. Tell her I wish her many years of happiness. Bye!"

When she turned towards the Triplets, she was smiling.

"That was your father. He wanted to be sure that you came home tomorrow," she told them.

"I guess Mother has been lonesome," murmured Iva, glad and sorry, too, because the visit was so nearly ended.

"We are having a very pleasant time, Aunt Mary, but Mother doesn't want us to wear you out, or our welcome, either," added Iona.

"She is awfully particular about our not missing any school, too. We haven't missed a day since we had the measles," Teddy explained.

Aunt Mary smiled again, and called up the stairs, "Rosemary darling, breakfast is ready. Are you coming?"

"I don't want any old breakfast," Rosemary called back.

Uncle Bill, who was entering the hall, heard her. He said, "I'll go see about her, Mary. You feed these hungry Baers."

There were brightly colored eggs for breakfast, but Aunt Mary did not return thanks, not even on that morning. Each of the Baers felt sorry. Presently Uncle Bill came in with Rosemary, who was smiling and apparently happy.

"Who's going to Sunday school?" he asked, when he had about finished his breakfast.

"I want to go, if you don't care," said Teddy.

"So do we!" spoke up Iona for herself and Iva.

"We haven't missed a single solitary Sunday in nearly three years. We promised our teachers we would be sure to go this morning," Teddy explained.

"I don't want to go!" declared Rosemary, pouting.

"You want to go on Easter morning to see all the beautiful flowers, Rosemary darling," her mother said, gently. "Why don't you begin this very morning and see if you can't make a good record like your cousins'?"

Rosemary looked at each one. Then she said, as she smiled, "I'd make a better one than they did!"

"That's the time!" exclaimed her father. "We'll all go this morning and see what sort of records we can make."

When they entered the assembly room at the church, the girls wanted to stand still and look. Such a profusion of beautiful flowers they had not seen in all their lives, except at florist shops. There were lilies and tulips and hyacinths. The air was sweet with their fragrance. Even the children and teachers and others looked like flowers in their bright, gay garments.

Since they had been old enough to love any Bible lessons, the Three Baers had loved the Resurrection Lesson. On this morning, they went with Rosemary to the Junior department. However, their Aunt Mary had to go along because Rosemary was almost as much of a stranger as they were.

It was during the closing exercises that the superintendent explained about the box of growing plants that had caught Teddy's eye.

"In this box," she explained, "I planted exactly fifty pansy seeds. I have taken excellent care of them and have watched with much interest as they began to grow. This morning I counted my tiny plants. Who can guess how many of the fifty seeds came up?"

From over the room came children's voices, like popcorn popping, guessing, guessing.

"There are thirty-six. Fourteen seeds did not grow. In each tiny seed there should have been life. Evidently fourteen seeds lacked life. I have learned a lesson from these pansy seed which I want to tell you. On this day we remember how the Lord Jesus arose from the dead. He had been laid in a tomb. But He did not stay there. He came back to life. When people die, we say we bury them. We say we plant seed. So I planted fifty seed, not knowing whether they had life in all of them or not. Fourteen did not have life. So this is the lesson I have learned. Many people live on and on and do not have Life in their hearts because they do not love the Lord Jesus and have never accepted Him as their Saviour, letting Him come into their hearts. These people are like the fourteen seed which did not grow. But boys and girls and men and women who love the Lord Jesus and who have opened their hearts to Him are like the thirty-six seed that had life in them and grew.

"Just suppose each one of you this morning was a seed and you were being planted. Would you grow as my thirty-six seeds did, or would you just lie in the ground and never grow at all? Each one is a seed in God's beautiful garden, which is the world. He wants every one to grow, to become the earnest Christians He knows you can become if you will only love Him and trust Him and obey Him. You who have already given your hearts to Jesus are growing even as He did when He was a little boy. You are becoming more and more like Jesus. Some day, when the time comes for you to die, you will go to be with Jesus in heaven. But maybe there are some other boys and girls here who are like the fourteen seeds that failed to grow. Those children have not let Jesus come into their hearts. I wonder if on this beautiful Easter morning there is some one, a girl or a boy, or even some grown-up visitor, who wants Jesus to come into your heart with His wonderful Life? Let's sing that chorus, 'Into My Heart,' shall we?"

Every one stood. They bowed their heads and closed their eyes and sang the song as a prayer.

"Now, if some little girl or boy wants Jesus really to come into your heart, will you come here and stand by me as we close our eyes and sing that chorus again?" asked the superintendent.

The Three Baers did not peep, but they felt and heard a slight movement and knew some one was opening his or her heart for Jesus to come in. Then the song ended. Iona hoped it was Rosemary. Iva hoped so, too. But it was not. It was two other little girls and an older boy.

On the way to the church auditorium, Teddy eased over to his sisters and said, "That was good. I'd like to know if Rosemary is a Christian."

"Yes, and I'd like to know about Aunt Mary," added Iona.

"And Uncle Bob," said Iva.

Teddy sat on one side of Uncle Bob with Rosemary between him and her mother while the girl triplets sat on the other side of Aunt Mary. How lovely the pulpit was with only masses of pure white lilies for decoration. The choir sang beautifully and the visitors enjoyed the song. Presently every one sang. The song was "Up From the Grave He Arose." Even Teddy held up his chin and sang that song, for they all loved it in his home.

After a while the minister was saying, "Have you ever wondered how the third robber may have felt? Barabbas was his name. If you had been in a dungeon, condemned to die, and had suddenly been led out into the sunshine and told that another man was taking your place and that you were free, how would you feel? Would you hate the man who took your place? Would you love him? Barabbas was a sinner, but he was human even as you and I. I can not help but think he must have been grateful to Him who was taking his place, dying on his cross. I can not help but think that he must have followed the people who went up Calvary's mountain. I believe he saw the precious body of the Lord Jesus laid in the tomb. I believe he saw the rock rolled before the tomb and sealed. I even like to believe that he stayed and kept watch, wondering what might yet take place. I like to think that Barabbas saw the empty tomb just as the woman and the disciples saw it. And I like to believe that he, the thief, believed. He believed because the Man Jesus had died in his place when he was the one who should have been crucified. He believed because he loved that Man.

"Hear me, on this glad morning, oh, my people! It was your cross as well as Barabbas' that Jesus bore up Calvary's mountain. He died for your sins as well as for that thief's. What will you do with this same Jesus? If you do not receive Him and give Him your heart, you are a thief also, for you are keeping from Him that which is rightly His. He paid for you. You belong to Him. You are not your own. What will you do with this Jesus who arose from that tomb and who loves you today as He loved you then?"

"I'm glad I'm not robbing Jesus," thought Teddy.

"I'm glad I'm not a thief," thought Iona.

"I'm glad I have given my heart to Jesus because I love Him," thought Iva.

Rosemary looked at her mother and at her father and wondered what they would do with Jesus. She wondered about her cousins. Did they all love Jesus? She did, but she didn't understand any of it very well.

And Aunt Mary was thinking that she did not love Jesus anything like as much as she would. She was going to be a much better Christian than ever she had been.

Uncle Bill sat very still and listened. What had he done with Jesus? A long time ago he had given his heart to the Lord Jesus. Then he had become so very busy earning a living for his family that he had neglected this Man who had carried the cross to Calvary for him. He was sorry. He was ashamed. From that very moment he was going to be a much better Christian.

On the way home he said to his visitors, "Well, and how did you like our church?"

"It's a very beautiful church," Teddy said, politely.

"It's bigger than our church at home," added Iona.

"Uncle Bill, did you mean the church house or the people and the preacher and the sermon and things like that?" asked Iva, seriously.

"That's it, Iva! You have it exactly right. There is a difference between a beautiful church and what goes on inside it. I'm glad you took me up on that. I honestly meant the services."

"Well, I liked the junior department lessons, especially about the pansy seeds," said Teddy. "I'm glad I have Life in me."

"Just what do you mean by that?" asked his Uncle Bill.

Then Teddy explained about the seed and how some did not grow.

"I see!" softly murmured Uncle Bill.

"I liked about Barabbas," Iona said. "I was glad I had given my heart to Jesus. Every one of us at home has. We ask the blessing before we eat and Daddy reads the Bible every night or we do, and then he or Mother prays every single night. Of course, we pray, too, when we go to bed and lots of times in the daytime, because Daddy doesn't know all the things we want to tell Jesus about."

Neither Uncle Bill nor Aunt Mary said anything for a moment. Then Uncle Bill did say, "Well, you must have thought you were among a pretty bad bunch when you came to see your Uncle Bill and Aunt Mary and no one even thought about asking the blessing."

"I thought about it," Iona almost whispered.

"What's the blessing?" asked Rosemary.

"Oh, Rosemary darling, when we really love the Lord Jesus, we are thankful to Him for every blessing we have, for our food especially. When we sit down at the table, we should bow our heads and thank the Lord for the good food He has helped us obtain," explained her mother.

"I want to ask the blessing!" announced Rosemary. "Next time we eat, I want to ask it!"

"You surely may do that, little daughter," said her father.

And that is how it happened that Rosemary did thank the Lord Jesus for the good dinner that they had that day.

In the afternoon, after they had all rested, Uncle Bill took the Three Baers on a long drive, giving them another sight of the mighty Atlantic ocean.

"Isn't is wonderful how the Lord Jesus keeps it from washing everything away?" asked Teddy. "He lets it come just so far and no farther."

"Isn't it wonderful!" repeated Rosemary, and sweetly, too.

7

HOMEWARD BOUND

MONDAY morning!

What a hurrying and scurrying there was to get the Three Baers up and off on a seven o'clock bus! They were going home, alone! Little shivers of excitement and delight chased up and down their spines. They did not pack their suitcases so carefully this time. They were going HOME! They did take time to make sure they were leaving nothing, for Mother Baer had said, "It is a dreadful nuisance to have guests leave something that must be wrapped and mailed to them. So do bring back everything you take, but nothing else! Be just as sure that you do not accidentally snatch up something that is not yours as you are to bring all that does belong to you." As if they would! They might, however, quite accidentally.

Finally they were on the bus, Iva and Iona together on a seat with Teddy directly in front of them. Each had a ticket tucked safely in a pocket or a purse. The bus door banged. On the sidewalk stood Aunt Mary and Uncle Bill and Cousin Rosemary, who was weeping lustily.

"I don't want them to go home!" she wept. "I want them to stay here!"

The huge car began to roll slowly away. The visiting Baers waved at the vanishing relatives, and saw Uncle Bill stoop to dry the tears from Rosemary's face. Then they settled in their seats, homeward bound!

"We've had a good time," sighed Iona. "But isn't Rosemary the strangest child you ever saw? The idea of her crying because she did not want us to go when she has acted all the time as if she were sorry we had come. She wouldn't let us touch her dolls and she snatched her books from Teddy and yet she didn't want us to leave!"

"She needs our Mother and Daddy hold of her for a while. She would have better manners then. She would behave herself, too, and not be so selfish and pouty. I just hope she does come to visit us next summer. She'll have some of that taken out of her, or I miss my guess," said Teddy, who had turned around to talk to his sisters.

"O Teddy, she has been sick a whole lot and it isn't really her fault she is so spoiled. If her mother and father hadn't given in to her the way they have, she would be different. I guess if our mother and daddy let us have our own way all the time we'd be spoiled, too. I think Rosemary is right sweet, sometimes," Iva said, trying to defend her delicate little cousin.

"Sweet, like fun!" muttered Teddy. "Even if she has been sick, she needn't be such a cry baby."

"But, Teddy, it's not all her fault, I say!" repeated Iva.

"Well, I don't care. She doesn't have to be so babyish," he insisted, as he turned back to gaze from his window.

"I hope I never have an only child!" Iva sighed, as she relaxed and rested her head against the soft cushions of her chair.

"Yes, and so do I! But if I do, I'm certainly not going to spoil her. I'll adopt her some brothers and sisters, rather than let her grow up all by herself and become selfish and cross. I'll get her some brothers and sisters from Europe where they are sending children to the United States!" Iona said.

"Maybe there won't be any old war in Europe by that time," Iva said, hopefully.

"Well, maybe. I certainly hope not. But I'll get some poor homeless children from some place. There certainly must be plenty of them."

Presently Teddy twisted himself until he was facing his sisters again. He said, "I liked Uncle Bill and Aunt Mary. They were grand to us. I liked what we saw of Florida, too. I'd like to go back some time when we could stay longer, like a Christmas vacation."

"That would be fun," agreed Iona. "I'll tell you what. Let's save our money and come back next Christmas!"

"All right! Let's! What do you say, Iva?" asked Teddy.

"I'm willing. We've each got a dollar to spend today for our dinner and supper. Maybe we could begin by saving some of that," Iva suggested.

"That's so! I'm not hungry, because I ate such a big breakfast. I could do with a 'hot dog' or two and just a little of something else for lunch and not much supper, because we could eat when we get home," offered Teddy.

"We have those sandwiches Aunt Mary gave us. Don't forget them," Iona reminded them.

"What did we do with the box?" asked Iva, as she began to search for it. "I thought we had it back here, but we haven't."

She and Iona bumped their heads together, looking for the box of lunch. They did not find it.

"Teddy, do you have it?" asked Iona.

Teddy looked. He did not have it!

"Oh, isn't that a shame! We must have left it in the car, though I do believe I remember Aunt Mary giving it to me. We could have saved a lot of money if we had those sandwiches," sighed Iona.

Just then Iva kicked something on the floor.

"Teddy, look under your seat and see what my foot hit," she said.

And sure enough, there was the box of sandwiches!

"Oh, goody!" they all exclaimed.

It was not long till the bus was full of passengers. A very nice looking young woman sat beside Teddy. She had not been sitting there long when she began to smoke a cigarette. Teddy was polite. He edged nearer his window, but he also wrinkled up his nose as he caught Iona's eye. And Iona made a face at Iva.

Before long Iva said, "I'm getting sick!"

"At your stomach?" asked Iona, anxiously.

"Yes! My head's aching, too. It's that old cigarette smoke."

Poor Iona! She looked at her ailing sister with sympathy. She wondered if it would be polite if she should ask the young woman please not to smoke because it made Iva sick.

Presently the driver stopped. He said, "Ten-minute stop here. Any one may get out and stretch who so desires."

What good news! The Three Baers were among the first to alight.

"I was getting awfully sick," Iva told the driver.

"Did you get car sick?" he asked, kindly.

"No, sir. I never was car sick. It was the cigarette smoke. It came right back in my face. This fresh air is making me feel better," she said, politely.

"Come in here and take a drink of good water. That will help, too," he suggested, for Uncle Bill had told him about the Three Baers and had asked him to take very special care of them.

That was a short ten minutes. When they were all seated again and the door closed, the driver stood beside his place and, facing the crowded car, said, "There will be a twenty-minute stop for lunch at twelve. You are requested kindly not to smoke while the bus is in motion. Please do your smoking during the rest stops. I thank you!"

Then he took his place and away went the bus.

"Isn't he a nice man!" exclaimed Iona to Iva.

"Yes, he is! I do hope Teddy will be as thoughtful and kind when he grows up."

"He will!" quickly assured Iva.

When the Three Baers had been watching for some little time the changing scenes from the bus windows, and were really becoming drowsy and very nearly sleepy, Teddy, squirming around in his seat until he could almost face his sisters, suggested, "Let's eat some of Aunt Mary's lunch now so we won't be hungry when we get out. Then we won't have to spend much of our money!"

"All right!" his sisters agreed, readily.

Iona opened the box very carefully, while Teddy managed to kneel in his seat and watch. Then with both hands full, he twisted back and began to eat his sandwiches while he looked from the window. When the bus did stop, there was not a single hungry Triplet! All they wanted was a drink of water! While the other passengers ate, they walked up and down the sidewalk near the bus, stretching their legs. Before it was time to start, the driver walked with them, chatting as if they were all the same age.

By the time they were again in their seats, the Baers and the driver, whose name they learned was Ted Stover, were good friends.

"He's nice!" softly Iona said to Iva. "He must be the very nicest bus driver there is."

"I guess he would win a medal or something if any one gave medals to bus drivers. Don't you?" Iva wanted to know.

Iona nodded her head, answering, "I'm sure he would. I wish we could go all the way with him, but he says he goes no farther than where we change buses at four. I hope another nice one is on that bus, but he won't be like this one."

Iva sighed and settled back against the cushion. Before many minutes she was asleep! Seeing that her sister slept, made Iona sleepy also. And she closed her eyes, just to rest them. The very first thing she knew, she was in a room full of babies and they all seemed somehow to belong to the Baer Family! The bus stopped. She awoke with a start just as she was about to try to pick up a third baby when she already had two in her arms! She looked at her sister and giggled.

"What's the matter?" Iona wanted to know.

"I had the funniest dream!" Iva told her, and then went on to tell what she had dreamed.

"Wouldn't it be funny, if it were true?" asked Iona, with a little shiver up and down her back. "Only I'd hate to have a whole roomful all at once."

"Roomful of what?" asked Teddy, who had overheard a little of what was being said.

"Babies!" laughingly both girls told him.

Teddy merely grunted and turned back to his window. Babies, indeed!

At four o'clock the big bus stopped at a bus station. The driver helped them from his car and said, "You'll have a layover of an hour here. Your northbound bus doesn't leave until five. Be sure to be here. It would be pretty terrible to have Three Baers left in this town all night!"

They all laughed and promised to be right there. Then he took them inside and showed them exactly where the bus would be announced and where it would be standing for departure.

"It isn't always that I have the opportunity of carrying Baers in my bus, and especially three at one time. I want to celebrate this occasion. How about a box of candy for you?" he asked, when he was ready to leave.

"Oh!" exclaimed the girl Baers. "That would be lovely."

"Do you like candy, Teddy?"

"Yes, Mr. Stover, I do!"

The box of candy contained a whole pound and was most politely and gratefully received. Then the very pleasant bus driver was gone and the Triplets were left alone in the waiting room. They sat and looked about them, feeling strangely alone.

"Shall we open our box of candy?" asked Iona, who was holding it.

"If you want to!" Teddy was ready any time!

Iva looked at the box and then at her brother and sister. She said, "I think it would be awfully nice to take it home just like that to show Mother and Daddy."

For only an instant Iona and Teddy hesitated before they agreed. The box was not opened.

"Let's go look at that map," finally Teddy suggested.

On a wall there hung a huge map of the southern States, showing the roads that crossed and recrossed everywhere.

"It looks like a spider's web," Iona said, as they gazed at it.

"Here's where we were and this is the way we are going," Teddy told them, as he traced the route on the big map.

While they were looking at it, trying to count the miles they had traveled, they heard some one near them talking strangely. They turned to see who it was. Near them was a woman and a little boy, about Teddy's age, though slighter. They were not talking English, but some foreign language. It sounded so strange to the American children that they had to watch and listen. The boy seemed frightened and the woman was trying to encourage him. Teddy wished he knew what was being said. Presently the woman caught Teddy's eye and smiled. He smiled back! Then she began to talk very fast, at least it seemed very fast to the three American children who were listening so closely, to the boy, and pointed to Teddy. The strange boy merely looked at Teddy with blank staring eyes.

"He is a stranger in America," the woman said to Teddy, in rather broken English. "He is afraid of the big bus he must ride in to go to my home."

The Three American Baers stepped slightly nearer the foreign boy. Smiling his broadest and most friendly smile, Teddy said, "Oh, it is fun! We've been on a bus ever since seven o'clock this morning, and we don't reach home till nine tonight. It's fun, really. You'll like it," he finnished, trying to make the boy understand.

The woman spoke again to the boy, gesticulating with her hands. The poor little boy looked again at the children, but he did not smile.

"You see, he is just from Poland. He is still afraid of the war," the woman explained.

"Oh!" said Teddy, sadly, and looked at his sisters, who were also looking very sad.

While they were talking, a man stepped up beside them. He asked, "Are you the Three Baers?"

The Three Baers looked at him in surprise. Teddy, being the "man," replied, "Yes sir! We are!"

The man lifted his hat from his head and bowed, as he said, smiling, "I am certainly pleased to meet you. And you are triplets?"

"Yes, we are, sir!" again Teddy answered, very politely.

"How old are you?"

"We are twelve years old, sir," again from Teddy.

The woman and little boy were listening. The woman spoke to the boy and he looked at the Triplets with more interest.

"It has been a long time since we have had Three Baers in our town. I wonder if you would mind stepping out upon the sidewalk so that I could snap a picture of you. You see, I am a reporter of our daily paper and I should like to have a little writeup and your picture in our paper," the man explained.

"Why, yes, sir, I suppose so. That is, if we don't miss our bus. It leaves at five. But it isn't five yet," Teddy said, glancing at a clock.

"Mister, why don't you take a picture of this little boy, too? He has come all the way from Poland and he is afraid because he has been in a dreadful war," Iona spoke up and said.

"Why, certainly!" agreed the man, kindly. "Are you his mother?"

The woman shook her head. "I am his mother's cousin. In this country I have been ten years now. His papa and his mama, they were killed in the war. Some kind neighbors, they send him over here. I take him to my home and he be my little boy now," she explained.

"By all means, please come out with the Baers!" exclaimed the newspaper man.

So out to the sidewalk they all went, Teddy close to the little Polish boy. Pictures were taken. Teddy told him where they had been and a whole lot about them. Before the children returned to the bus station, Iona whispered to Iva and Teddy. Then she stepped up to the Polish boy, handed him the pound box of candy, and said, "Here!"

Slowly the boy accepted the gift. The woman spoke to him. She must have said, "Candy!" His face brightened, and he smiled. He said something which his cousin told them meant "Thank you!"

Then, before they knew it, five o'clock had come and the northbound bus was called. They waved at the little Polish boy and his cousin and ran to their bus.

"That was fun!" exclaimed Iona, as she settled in the new seat.

"Yes, it was!" agreed Teddy. "And I'll tell you what. I'm certainly glad I'm an American!"

"So'm I! I felt so sorry for that poor little Polish boy," sighed Iva. "And just to think maybe there are hundreds and thousands of children just like him in Europe."

"Won't we have the most to tell Mother and Daddy!" said Iona, as the bus gained speed. "I can hardly wait "

8

HOME!

TEDDY yawned. He stretched in his seat. It was eight o'clock. The rest of the lunch Aunt Mary had given them had been eaten. They were all just a little wee bit hungry, oh, quite a little bit, but not a Baer had spent a cent of his or her dollar! Teddy was growing sleepy. Sitting still and riding had made him sleepy. He twisted around till he could see his sisters. Iva was asleep. Iona looked almost asleep.

"It's five minutes past eight," he told her. "You'd better wake up Iva. You'd better keep awake yourself. The old bus might not put us off when we get home."

"Well!" Iona said, and yawned. Then she punched Iva.

"Are we home?" asked Iva, rubbing her eyes.

"No, but we are almost there," Teddy told her. "You'd better stay awake so we won't get left."

"All right," agreed Iva, and stretched all she could in a seat in a bus.

But it was so very, very difficult to keep awake fifty-five whole long minutes! Several times they all three dozed.

Then they would awaken with a jerk and shake one another until all three were once more awake. Finally it was five minutes till nine. Four minutes! Three minutes! Two minutes! One! Nine o'clock!

But the bus kept on going!

Teddy turned around again to his sisters, who were sitting very still and straight, trying to see from the windows out into the darkness. There was nothing that looked like their city outside.

"Are we on the wrong bus, Teddy, do you suppose?" asked Iona, half frightened.

"I don't know," slowly admitted Teddy. "But the driver saw our tickets. He wouldn't let us get on this bus if it were not the right one."

"Maybe we're late," Iva offered, almost in tears.

"It's five minutes after nine!" Teddy told them.

Just then the bus began to go through what looked like streets of a city, for there were many lights outside. The Three Baers sighed with relief. Surely this was the right bus. Surely this was HOME! And the bus was stopping. The driver turned in his seat and smiled at the Three Baers. He nodded, as he called the name of their very own city!

Iona was out first and jumped almost right into Daddy Baer's beloved arms. Then Iva. Then Teddy.

"We've had the best time!" they all tried to tell him at once.

"I am glad of that," Daddy Baer told them, happily, as he helped them and their suitcases into the car.

"Where's Mother?" asked Iva, when she did not see her dearest Mother in the automobile.

"She is waiting for you at home. She has a little surprise for you," Daddy Baer said, and smiled the jolliest and happiest they had ever seen him.

Iona and Iva exchanged glances and Teddy grinned. The girls giggled and hugged each other.

"Hurry, Daddy!" coaxed Iona.

"Don't hurry him!" Teddy said. "You'll know soon enough!"

"Oh, I can hardly wait!" Iona cried, as she tried to sit still.

"We had our pictures taken with a little boy all the way from Poland when we changed buses at four o'clock, Daddy," Teddy told his father. "He was here all by himself because his father and mother were both killed in the war. He was going home with his mother's cousin. He was afraid to ride in the big bus. I felt sorry for him."

"We gave him a big box of candy the first bus driver had given to us which we were saving to bring home to you and Mother," explained Iona. "But we thought you'd rather we gave it to him. Wouldn't you, Daddy?"

"Yes, indeed, I would! I'm glad that my cubs thought of doing that. Who took the pictures?"

Then Teddy told him all about the newspaper man. Daddy Baer did drive a little faster than usually he did, but he drove very carefully even then. They were entering their own driveway before the Three Baers had time to wonder where they were.

"Let's leave the suitcases here. I'll get them after awhile. Your Mother is very anxious to see you just as soon as she can," he said, as he opened the door for his daughters.

Teddy started to run ahead. Suddenly he stopped and stepped back beside his father. He had changed his mind about rushing into the house. They went in the back way, through the kitchen. A strange woman was in there.

"Here are the cubs, Tilly," Daddy Baer said, joyfully. "All home, safe and sound, and top-side up!"

Tilly had rosy cheeks and fair hair that she wore in two braids that were wound around her head. She was much plumper than Aunt Mary had been. She smiled. She said she was glad to see them.

"Where's Mother?" asked Iva, as they left the kitchen.

"We'll find her," promised her father, taking her hand.

Teddy followed last. Daddy Baer led them upstairs instead of into the living room. He led them straight to their mother's bedroom door.

"Maybe you had better not make too much noise," he warned, as he stopped with his hand on the door knob.

Then he opened the door, very slowly and very quietly Iona tip-toed in.

Iva tip-toed also.

Teddy swallowed a big lump that came up into his throat and followed his sisters on his tip-toes.

Mother Baer was lying in her bed!

"Mother!" cried Iona, and almost choked because she was so frightened and sorry to see her mother in bed.

Mother Baer held out her arms to her triplets and smiled a most joyful smile that seemed to make her whole face glow.

"My darlings!" she cried, as she kissed the girls and then Teddy, who had lingered a little in the back, trying to find something he was expecting to see in the room.

The girls looked also. They exchanged glances with each other, glances which asked, "Where?"

Then Mother Baer said, oh, so sweetly, "Look what Mother and Daddy have for you!" as she gently lifted back the cover from beside her.

And there!

A tiny baby!

"O Mother!" softly cried Iona.

"A baby!" almost whispered Iva, as she stood beside Iona and looked with wide eyes.

"Is it a little old girl?" asked Teddy, his voice husky.

"Teddy, it's a boy!" Daddy Baer said, as he placed his arm across his older son's shoulder. "A brother for you, son!"

"O Daddy! That's grand! Say, Mother, do you care if I give a yell?" asked Teddy, his face all smiles for the first time. "I feel one coming!"

"Don't yell too loud, Teddy," his mother said, laughing softly. "You might wake up your little brother, and he'd yell, too. He has a most excellent pair of lungs."

"I've got a brother!" cried Teddy, joyously, as he hopped lightly about the room.

"I guess we've got a brother, too," Iona told him.

"You can have him as long as he is a little ol' baby, but when he's big enough to play and know something, he's mine! I'm certainly glad he's not a little ol' girl!" Teddy told her.

"What's his name, Mother?" Iva asked, lovingly, as she still gazed upon the small, sleeping face.

"Let's call him Robert, for his father," suggested Mother Baer.

"Of course!" agreed his sisters.

"Bob and Ted!" pronounced Teddy. "That's what our names will be."

After a while when Bobby awoke and discovered he was hungry and they had all seen him fed and had even held him a tiny minute, the Three Baers discovered they, too, were hungry.

"Tilly will give you a snack," Mother Baer told them.

Tilly gave them each a glass of cold, sweet milk with bread and butter and Boysenberry jam.

As they ate, Teddy asked, "Well, now what'll we do about going to Florida next Christmas? Bob won't be big enough to make that long trip."

"That's so!" exclaimed Iona.

"What'll we do with all our money? We've each got a dollar," Teddy asked next.

For a moment the girls were silent. Then Iva said, slowly, "I'll tell you what. When we were born Aunt Iona and Aunt Iva and Uncle Teddy put five dollars for each of us in the bank and every time we've had a birthday, they've put in some more money for us. It's our education money. If no one puts in any for the new baby, he won't have any education money. So let's save up till we get two more dollars and put his five dollars in the bank along with ours. We wouldn't want to have an education and not have him have one, too."

Teddy studied the suggestion a minute as he ate his last bite of bread and butter and Boysenberry jam. Then, when he had swallowed his last drop of milk, he said, "That's as good a thing to do as I can think of. We can give a lecture on Florida and show our postcards down in the basement and charge to get in. Then when we open our curbstand again, we'll soon have five dollars. We're years and years older'n Bobby is. Every time he has a birthday we can put some more money in the bank for him. What do you say, Iona?"

"Why, I think it is a perfectly elegant idea!" agreed Iona. "It's a whole lot better than eating up our dollars would have been."

"We'll pray every day that our little baby brother will grow in wisdom and stature, and in favor with God and man just like the Bible says Jesus did," Iva added.

"We've got a lot of responsibility now. It wasn't so bad with Teddy for a brother because he was just the same age, but sisters are so responsible for brothers," Iona said, and yawned sleepily.

"That's so!" agreed Iva, seriously. "We have to be examples to our brothers. We'll have to help him grow up to be as nice as that bus driver was, or Uncle Bill, or Daddy!"

"You girls make me sick!" Teddy said, as he arose. "I guess Bob can take care of himself. If he can't, I guess I'll be his big brother and can show him how. Of course, you girls can help in lots of little ways, but he'll always want his big brother most. You just see!"

Tilly smiled. Then she said, "Your father said you had better go to bed now."

"Let's take just one more peep at our little brother and Mother," suggested Iva, as they started from the kitchen. "It's been the most wonderful Easter in the whole country."

"Yes, it has!" agreed Iona, while Teddy thought so too, but said nothing.

THE END